P9-CNH-248

C.2

COMPLIMENTS OF
CURRICULUM & INSTRUCTION

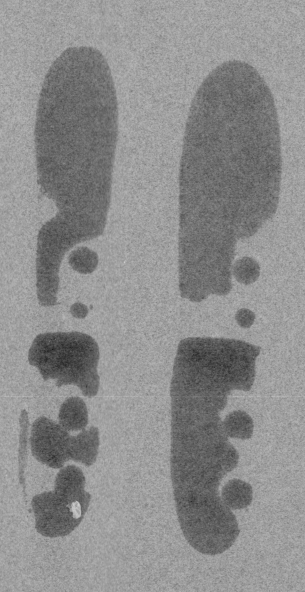

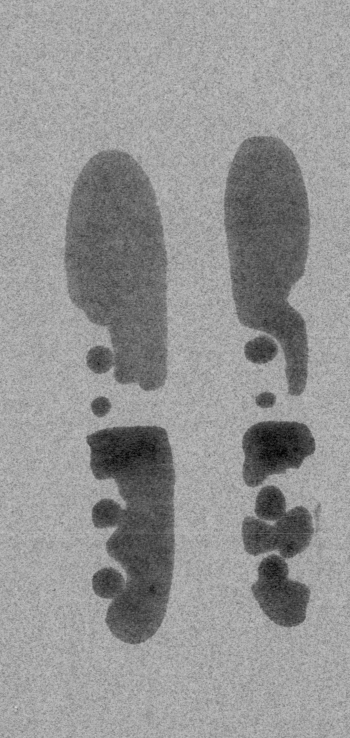

YONDER

by Tony Johnston • *pictures by* Lloyd Bloom

Dial Books for Young Readers   *New York*

Las Virgenes Unified School District
Willow Elementary School Library

Published by Dial Books for Young Readers
A Division of NAL Penguin Inc.
2 Park Avenue
New York, New York 10016

Published simultaneously in Canada by Fitzhenry & Whiteside Limited, Toronto
Text copyright © 1988 by Tony Johnston
Pictures copyright © 1988 by Lloyd Bloom
All rights reserved
Design by Atha Tehon
Printed in the United States of America
First Edition
W
1 3 5 7 9 10 8 6 4 2

Library of Congress Cataloging in Publication Data
Johnston, Tony. Yonder.
Summary: As the plum tree changes in the passing seasons,
so do the lives of a three-generation farm family.
[1. Seasons—Fiction. 2. Country life—Fiction. 3. Family life—Fiction.]
I. Bloom, Lloyd, ill. II. Title.
PZ7.J6478Yo 1988 [E] 86-11549
ISBN 0-8037-0277-9
ISBN 0-8037-0278-7 (lib. bdg.)

The art consists of oil paintings that
are reproduced in full color.

For my grandparents, Addie Pearl, David Taylor, and Utah Taylor—Capital Yonder. And for Charlotte Zolotow   T.J.

To my last painting teacher and dear friend, Ronald Markman   L.B.

Yonder is the farmer on a jet black horse.
Yonder are the hills that roll forever.
Yonder is the river that runs to sea.
Yonder. Way over yonder.

There comes the farmer with a brand-new bride,
Riding down the hills that roll forever.
Digs a hole and plants a tree and says a prayer.
There. Just over there.

There is the cabin made of fine pine planks,
Filling up with cats and dogs and children.
Farmer plants a tree for every child who's born.
There. Just over there.

There come the neighbors down the dust-deep road,
Wagon creaking with a load of lumber.
Hammering and sawing till they build a barn.
There. Just over there.

There is the plum tree growing year by year,
Pink with clouds of blossoms in the springtime.
Daughter swinging up and up to kick the sky.
There. Just over there.

Inside is the mother by a quilting frame.
Outside is the father plowing wheat fields.
Children walk to school beneath a soft spring rain.
Dreaming. Dreaming of summer.

Children feed the chickens as the sun comes up.
Father milks the cow while cats are watching.
Feed the pigs and feed the geese and feed the goat.
There. Just over there.

There is the plum tree growing year by year,
Loaded with the fruit of early summer.
Young man makes a cradle in the old tree's shade.
There. Just over there.

There are the sons, now taller than the farmer.
There is a daughter at her wedding.
Neighbors come from near and far to fill the churchyard.
There. Just over there.

Brother pounding fence posts in the noonday heat.
Woodpeckers are pecking out the same song.
Everybody splashing when the work is done.
There. Just over there.

By and by the mother has become a grandma.
By and by the father is a grandpa.
Holding hands together as the sun goes down.
Going, going—gone!

Grandpa tells a story full of make-believe.
Lap is full of children in their nightshirts.
Owls are listening. Bears are listening. *What then? What?*
There. Just over there.

There is the plum tree growing year by year,
Glowing like a bonfire in autumn.
Pumpkins on the front porch grin from ear to ear.
There. Just over there.

Christmastime has come again. The snow falls down.
Grandma knitting caps and scarves and mittens.
Merry voices ringing through the frozen woods.
Joy! Joy to the world!

Grandpa knows a place with trees like tall white ships,
Standing on the hills that roll forever.
Bring one home, it fills the house with pine and wonder.
There. Just over there.

There is the plum tree growing year by year.
Leaves are gone, birds are gone in winter.
Wild deer walk beneath it as quiet as the snow.
There. Just over there.

There is the old man who was once a farmer,
Resting with a sleepy dog beside him.
Snoring in and out like a thousand, thousand bees.
There. Just over there.

There is the family beside the tree.
Neighbors come from near and far to be there.
Grandpa's dead. Grandpa's gone. So they plant a tree.
There. Just over there.

Yonder is the farmer on a jet black horse.
Yonder are the hills that roll forever.
Plum tree is in blossom with a thousand, thousand bees.
Yonder. Way over yonder.